For Jordan and Catherine,
who asked me to tell them a story.

Illustrations by
Nidhi Chanani

MISTY
THE PROUD CLOUD

Hugh Howey

Misty lived in the sky,
high above the mountains.

There was a valley nearby with a lake,
and a village where Misty and her
friends liked to play.

One bright blue day, Misty
and her friends decided to put
on a show for the people in the valley.

Jimmy became a locomotive.
A great plume of smoke
trailed from his stack.

Tonya made herself into a gazelle,
leaping clear across the valley.

Carlos turned into a wizard with a great flowing beard.

Karen looked like a fearsome
smoke-breathing dragon.

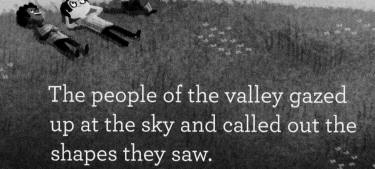

The people of the valley gazed up at the sky and called out the shapes they saw.

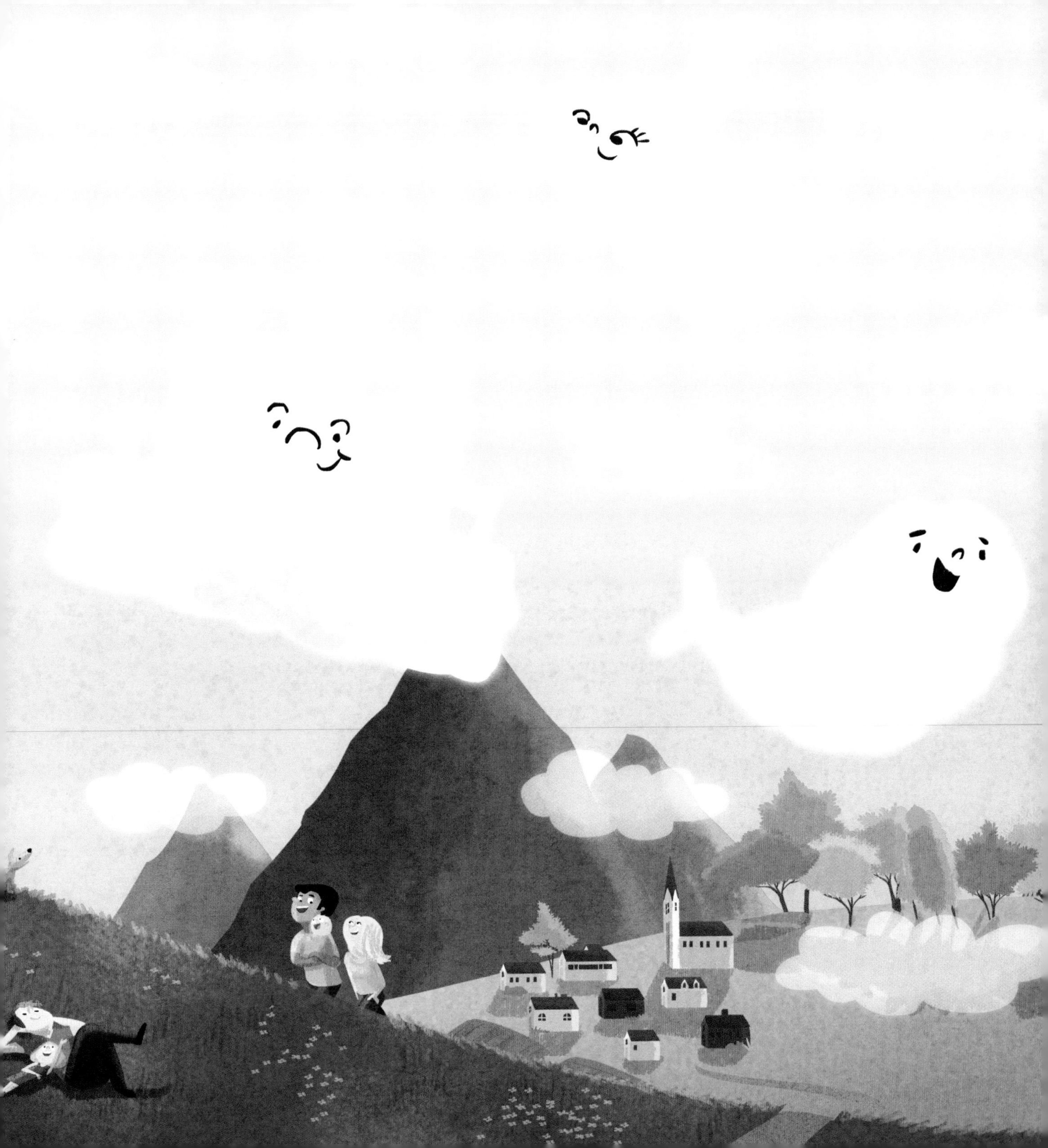

Misty desperately wanted to be
something different, so she tried
to change into a flower.

But she looked lumpy.

She tried to take the shape
of an oak tree, a leaf, even a
simple acorn.

She wanted to be an eagle,
tried to be a baby sparrow, but
couldn't even turn into an egg.

Everywhere she looked
her friends were becoming
something strange and new.

But Misty was just a plain old cloud.

She grew sad and gray and drifted off alone to cry.

Misty's father swooped in after her.
"What's the matter?" he asked.

"I can't be a dragon or a butterfly or a steaming locomotive," Misty sobbed.

Down below, the spring flowers bloomed from Misty's tears.

Gardeners were grateful for the nourishing rain.

The lake was full again.
Waterfalls spilled and the
fish leaped.

"Look," her father said,
pointing back to the valley.
"Look at how happy you make
them by being a cloud."

Misty drifted up the valley and saw that her father was right.

Birds and butterflies bounced from flower to flower, drinking nectar.

he spotted a
armer in a field,
oiling in the heat.
he lent him some
hade.

The farmer looked up at
her, wiped the sweat from
his brow, and smiled.

He was happy.

And Misty was too.